POTATO CHIP B

SO GOOD YOU CAN'T STOP READI

Get Up

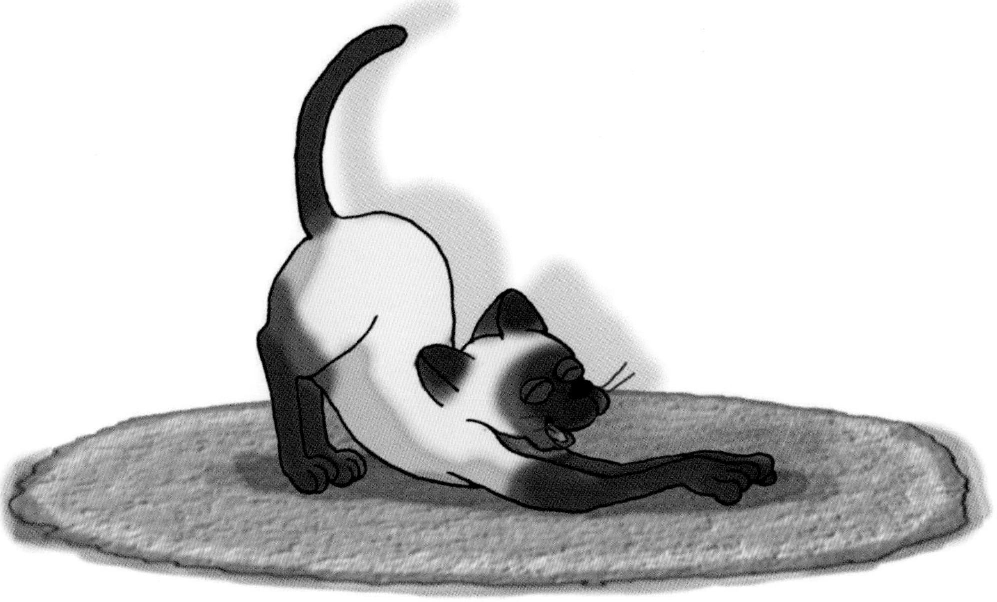

Written by Marilyn Pitt & Jane Hileman
Illustrated by John Bianchi

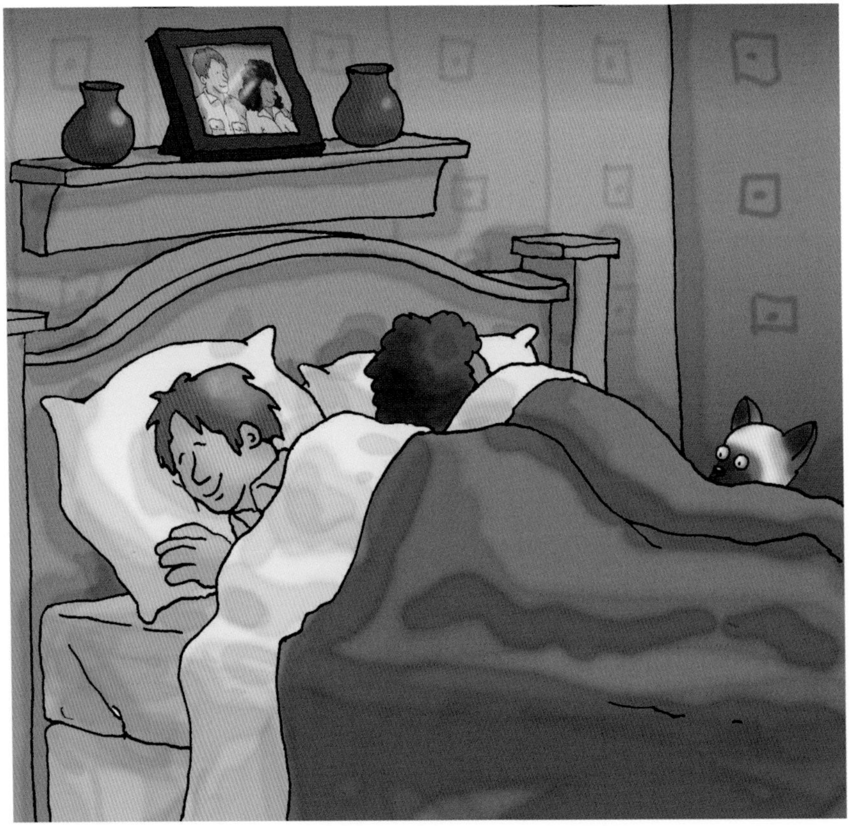

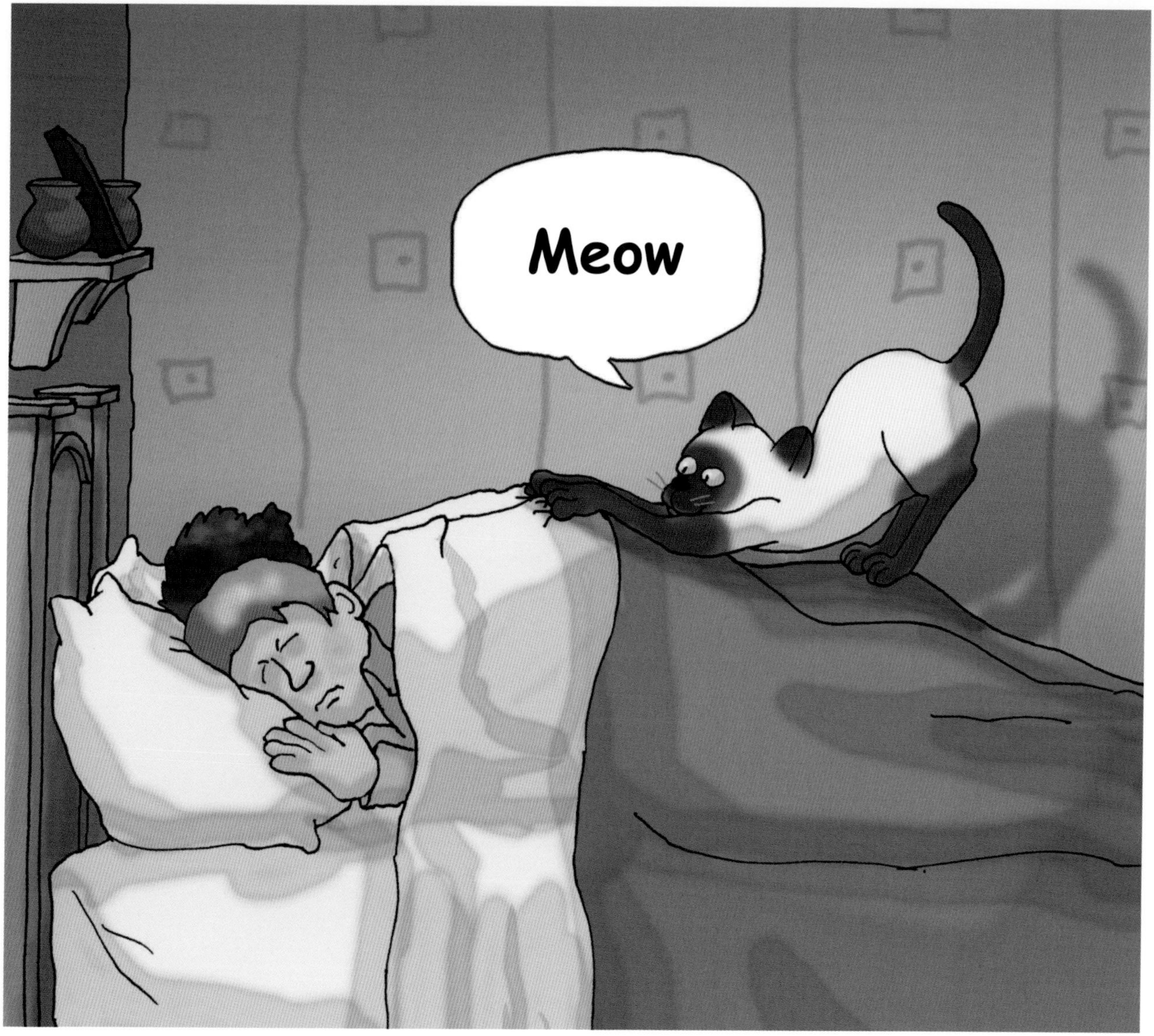

Get up.

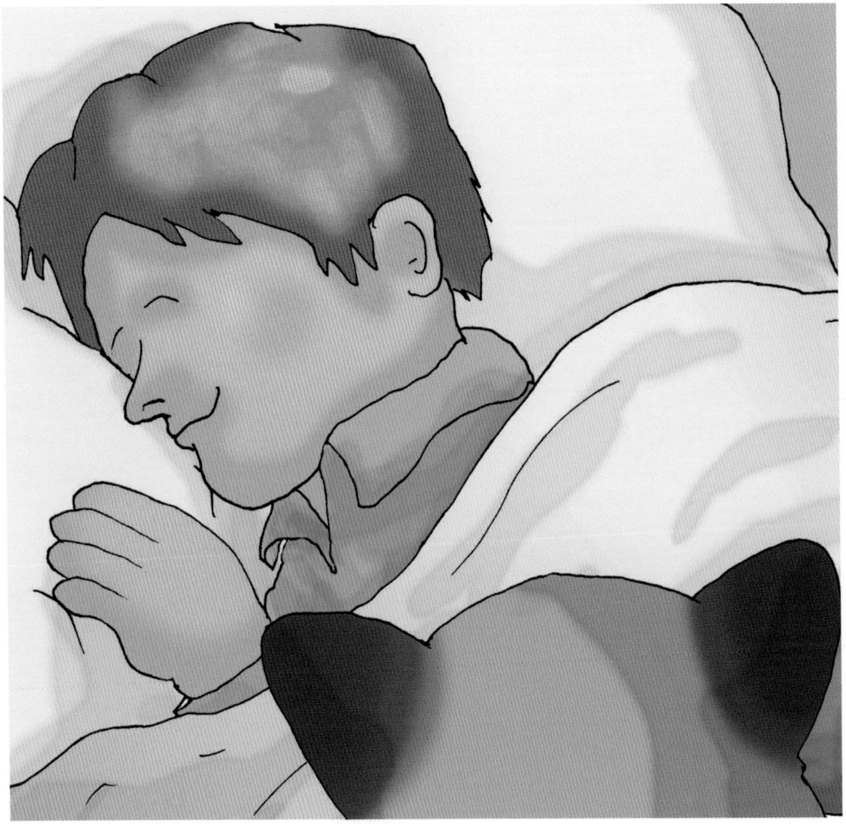

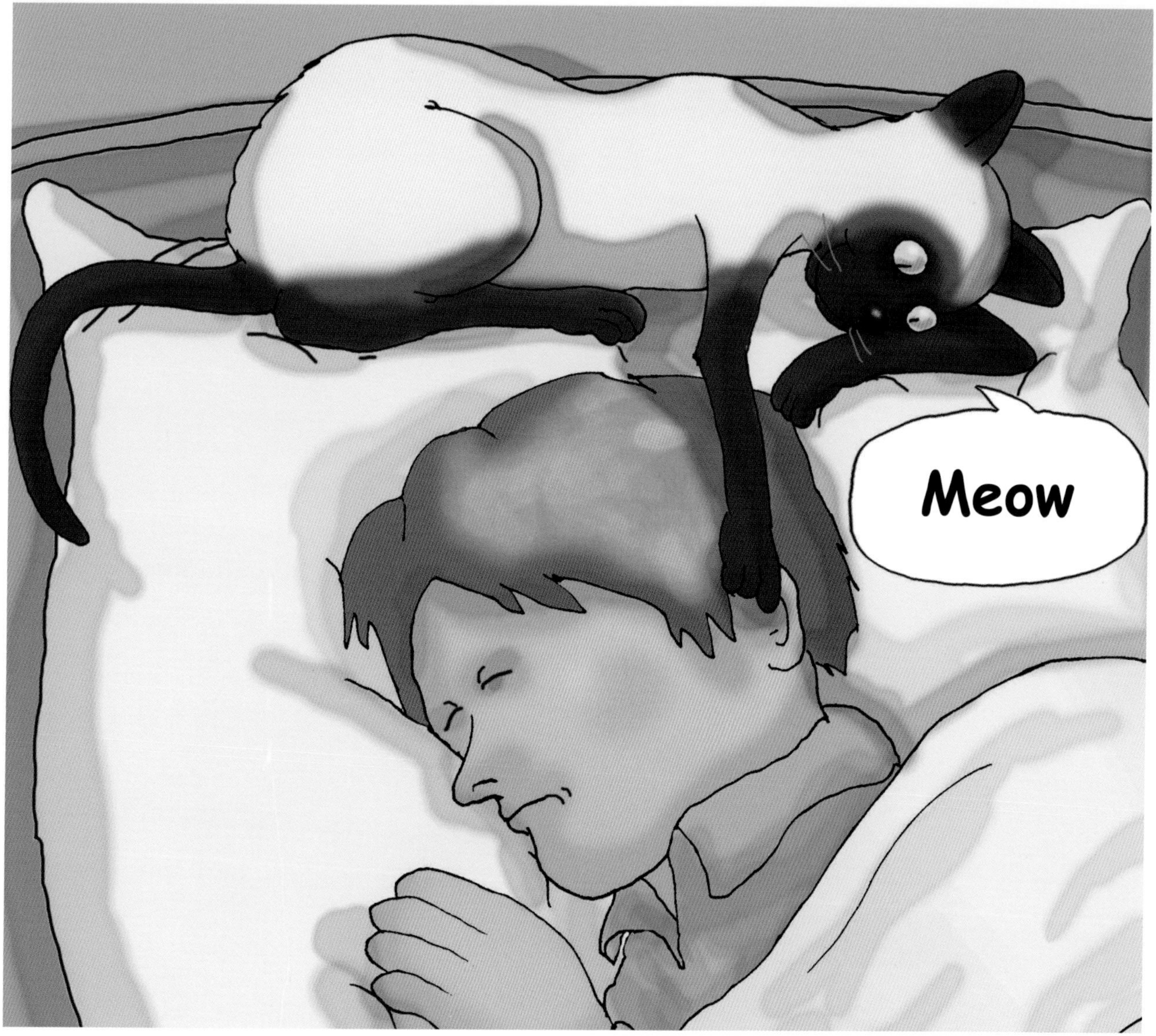

Get up.

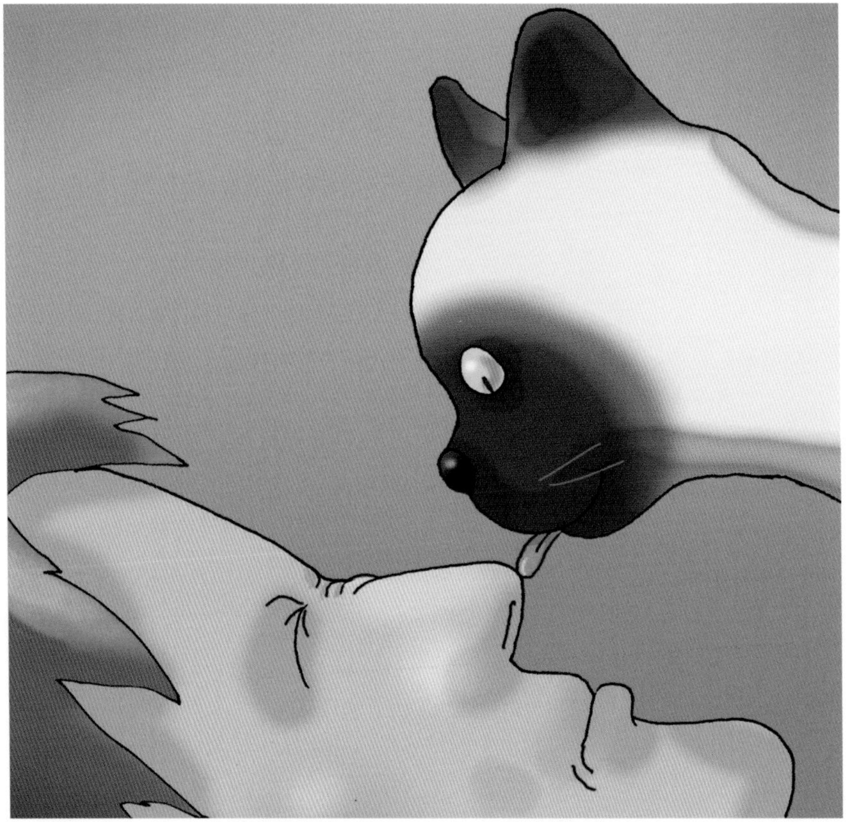

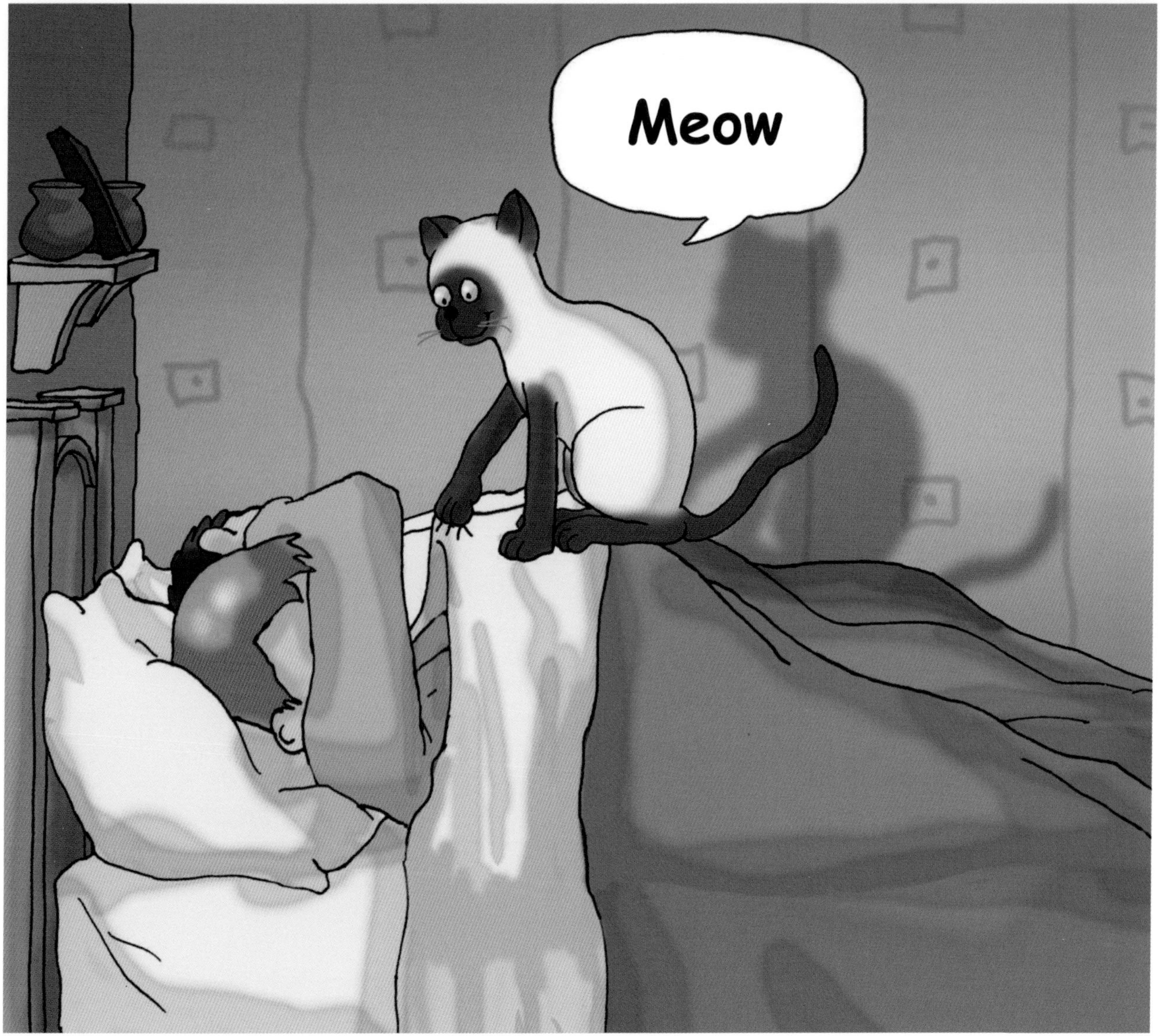

I want you to get up.

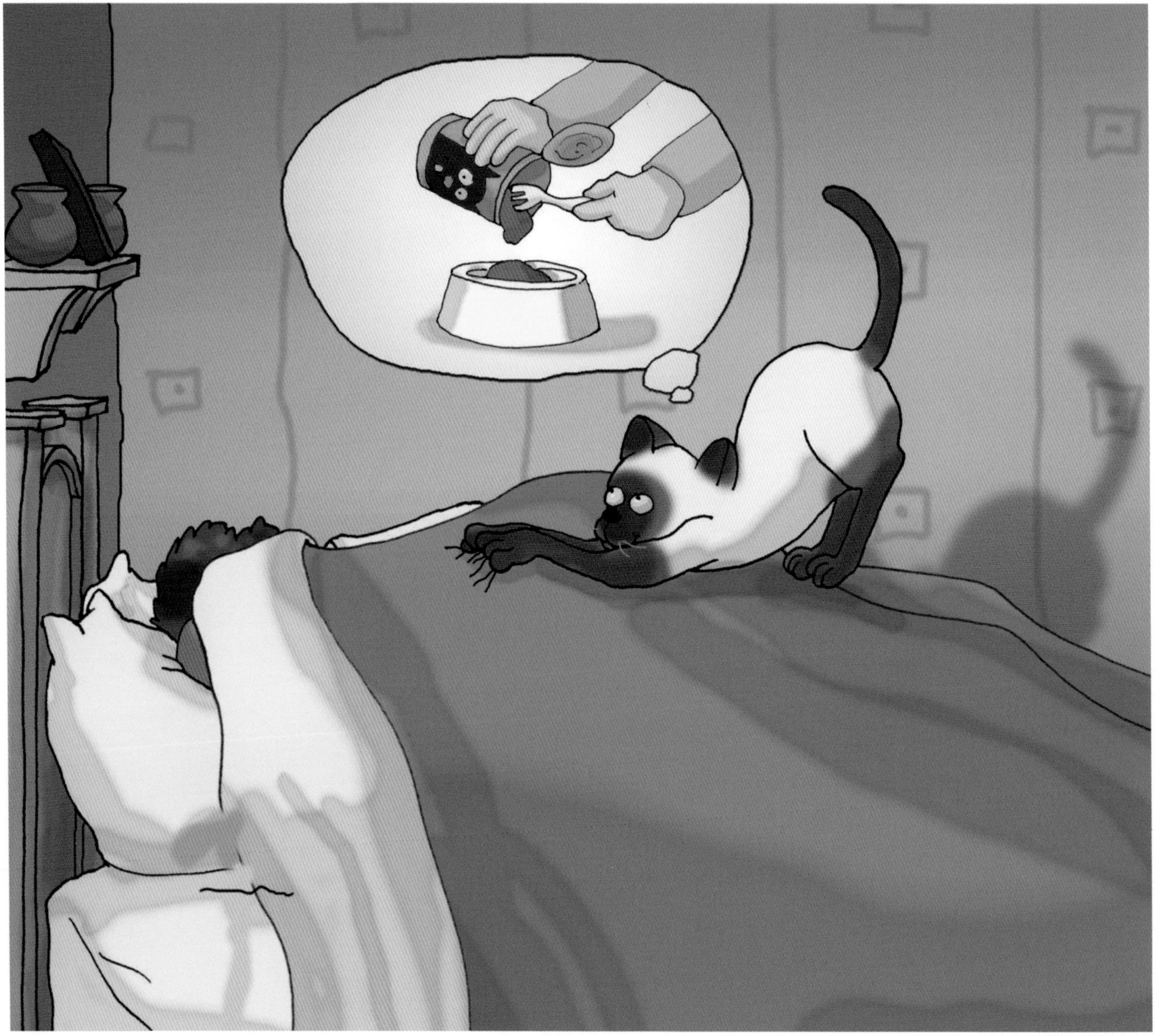

Get up. I want to eat.

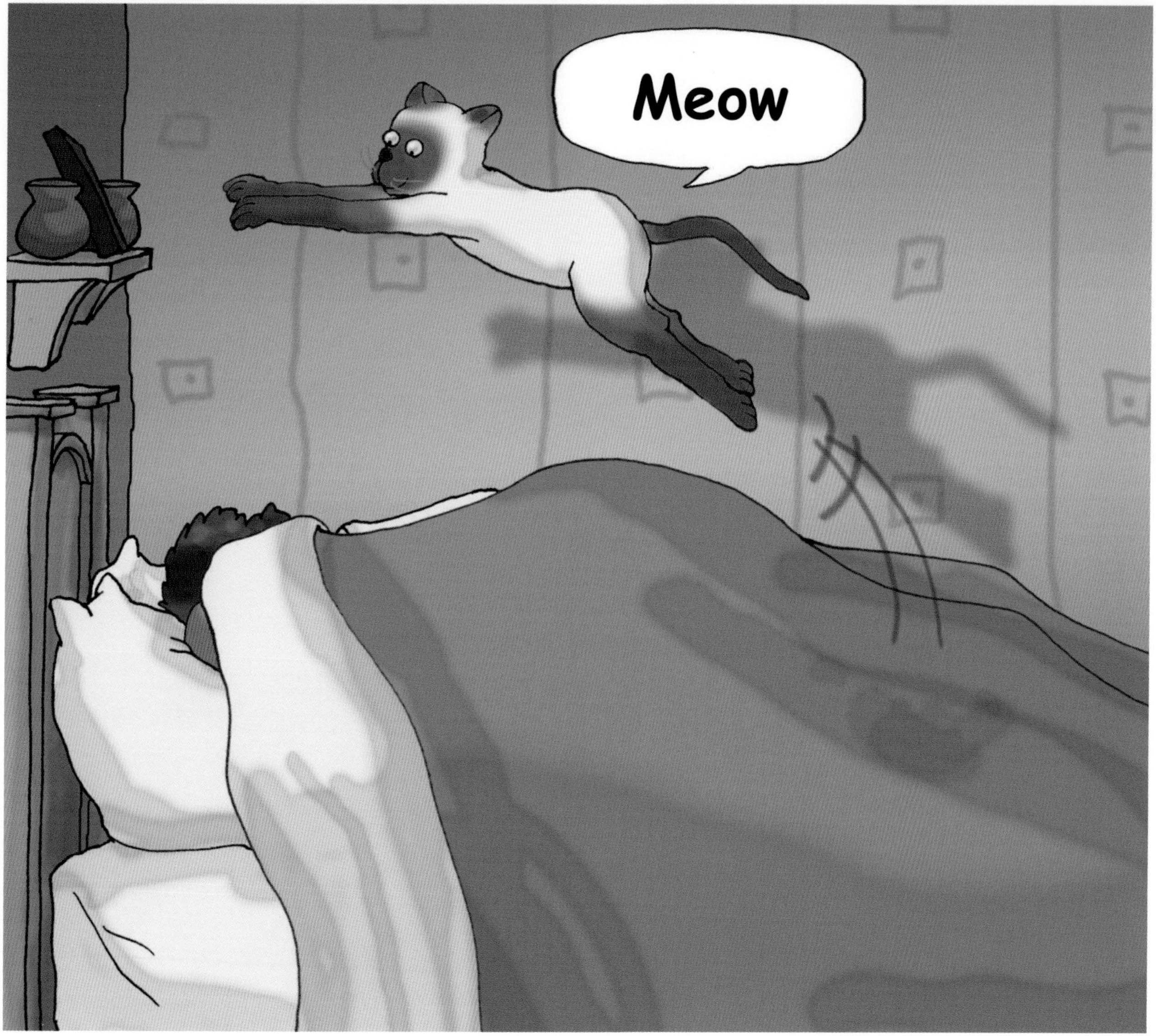

Come on. Get up.

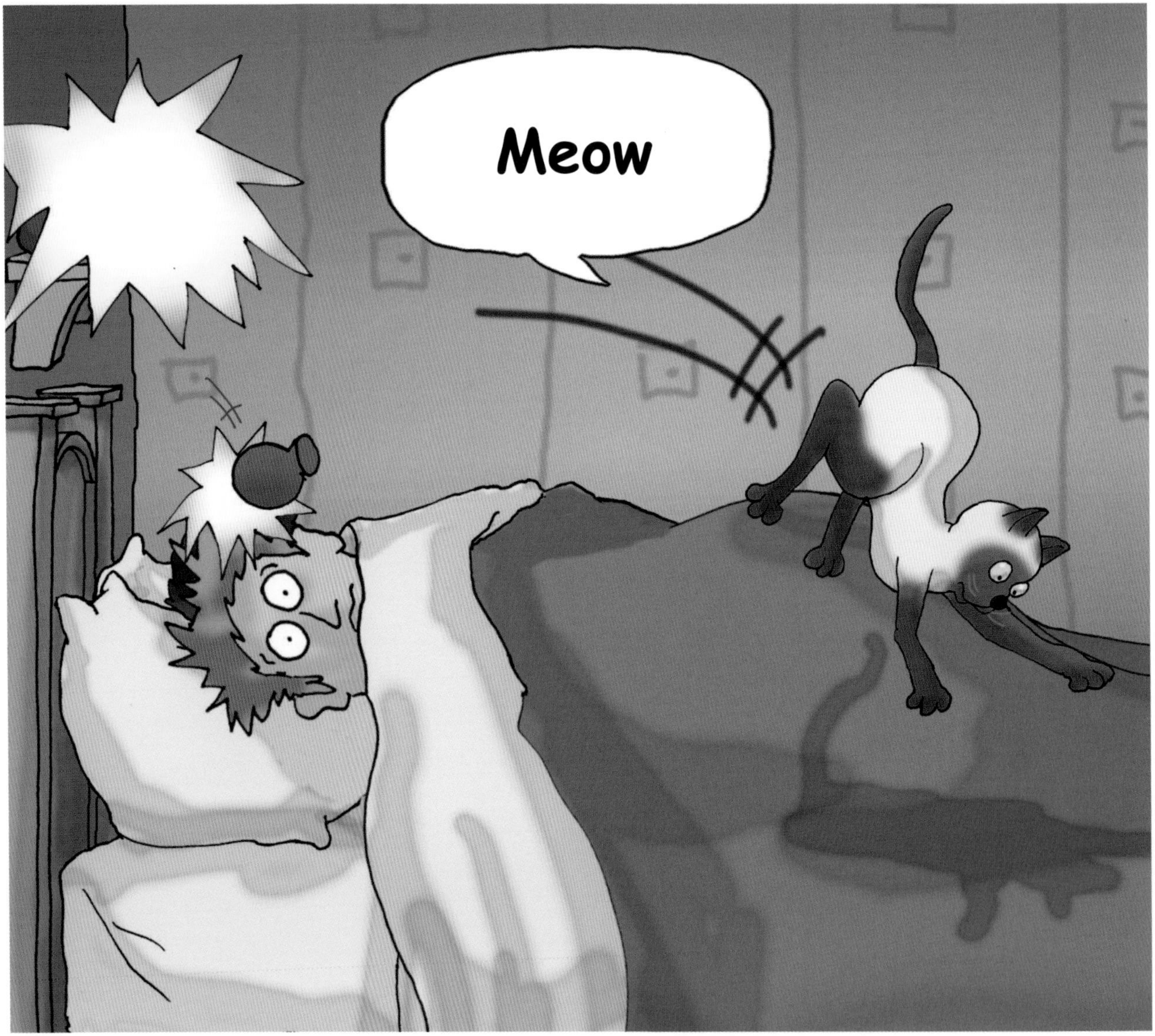

You have to get up.

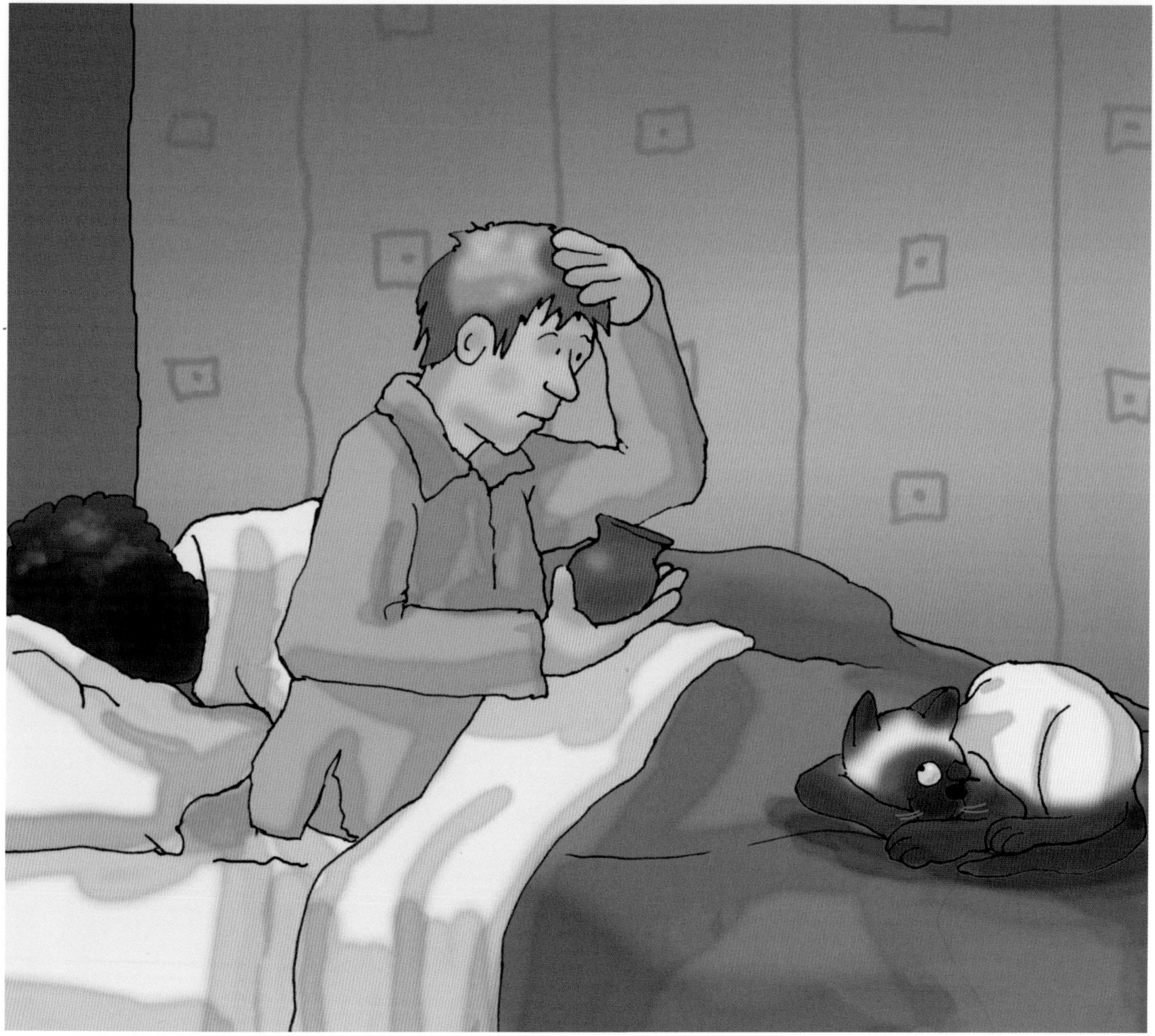

What is this?

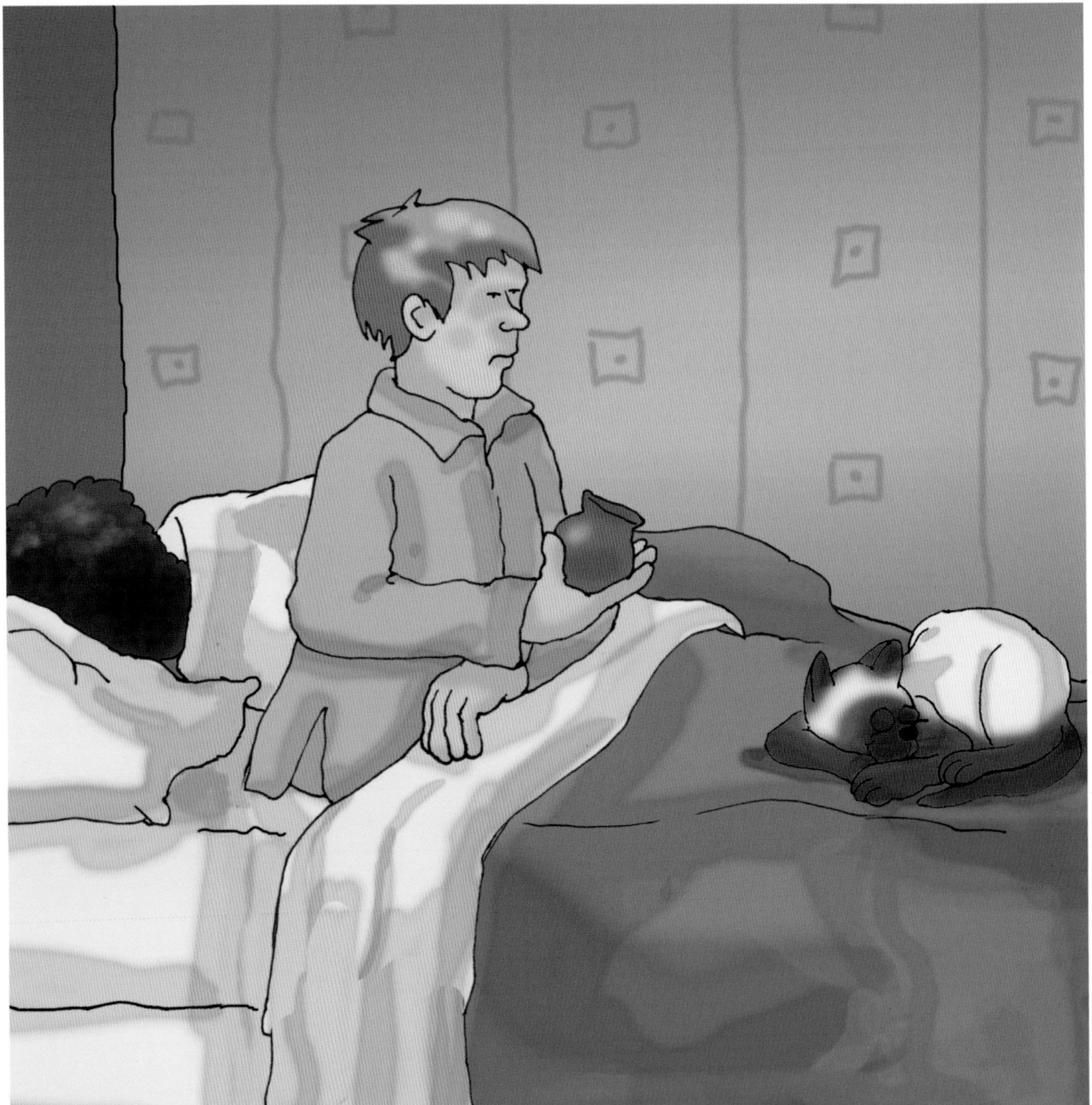